November 2007

To Lauren.

Rascal had so much fun in the pine forest at the Grand Canyon.

Sylvester Allred

Lauren —
Enjoy Rascal's
ad...

Diane Iverson

Rascal, the Tassel-Eared Squirrel

Happy Thanksgiving, Lauren
2007

With love,
Grandpa & Grandma

Rascal, the Tassel-Eared Squirrel

by Sylvester Allred

Illustrated by Diane Iverson

GRAND CANYON ASSOCIATION

Grand Canyon Association
P.O. Box 399
Grand Canyon, AZ 86023-0399
(800) 858-2808
www.grandcanyon.org

Printed in China
Edited by Todd R. Berger
Designed by Ron Short

First Edition
11   10   09   08   07   1   2   3   4   5

Library of Congress Cataloging-in-Publication Data

Allred, Sylvester, 1946–
   Rascal, the tassel-eared squirrel / by Sylvester Allred ; illustrated by Diane
Iverson. -- 1st ed.
        p. cm.
   Summary: Through the course of one year, a squirrel and her little brother are
born, explore their home in Grand Canyon National Park, learn to take care of
themselves, and grow to adulthood. Includes facts about the animals and plants
of the Grand Canyon region.
   ISBN-13: 978-0-938216-88-9 (alk. paper); 978-0-938216-44-9 (pbk.; alk. paper)
   ISBN-10: 0-938216-88-0 (alk. paper); 0-938216-44-9 (pbk.; alk. paper)
  1. Kaibab squirrel--Juvenile fiction. [1. Kaibab squirrel--Fiction. 2. Squirrels--
Fiction. 3. Seasons--Fiction. 4. Grand Canyon National Park (Ariz.)--Fiction.]
I. Iverson, Diane, ill. II. Title.
   PZ10.3.A437Ras 2007
   [E]--dc22
                                        2006038934

*It is the mission of the Grand Canyon Association to cultivate knowledge, discovery,
and stewardship for the benefit of Grand Canyon National Park and its visitors.
Proceeds from the sale of this book will be used to support the educational goals of
Grand Canyon National Park.*

Dedication

Rascal, the Tassel-Eared Squirrel is dedicated to my children, James and Rachel. I'm sure you both remember all the "Tuck Me In Like a Squirrel" bedtime stories that I used to tell you. And to my granddaughters, Annissa and Abigail. I look forward to sharing those bedtime stories with you. Last in line of mention, but first in my heart, is my wife, Donna.

—Sylvester Allred

This book is dedicated to my children, Kristin, Michele, and Rob, and to my grandchildren Aaron, Brycen, Rob, Tyler, Vanessa, and Victoria. Also, and especially, it is dedicated to Doug, my wonderful husband and hiking partner. May you always be good stewards of the earth's bounty.

—Diane Iverson

Acknowledgments

Special thanks and appreciation go to our spouses, Donna and Doug, who certainly deserve much credit for manuscript editing; helpful suggestions; supporting roles at home, in the field, and on the road; and for their heartfelt love. Thanks also to Todd Berger, our editor; Pamela Frazier, our publisher; Ron Short, our designer; and the rest of the staff at the Grand Canyon Association for their enthusiasm about and support of this project.

Two fascinating squirrels live across the Grand Canyon from each other.

They are both tassel-eared squirrels, with tufts of fur on the tips of their ears. The Abert's

squirrel lives on the South Rim. The Kaibab squirrel lives on the North Rim.

This book celebrates the four seasons of the first year in the life of Rascal,

a tassel-eared squirrel living in the ponderosa forests of Grand Canyon National Park. The life

of a tassel-eared squirrel is hard. It must rely on the forest to survive.

Spring

High in the trees of Grand Canyon's ponderosa forest, a female tassel-eared squirrel named Mother bounds along a highway of branches. She leaps easily from tree to tree. In a cheerful announcement of spring, the song of a tiny canyon wren drifts up from a rocky ledge in the canyon. The squirrel hurries along, looking for the perfect tree.

It is time to build a nest where Mother can raise her family. She finds a mighty ponderosa that splits into two trunks high above the ground. A dense crown of branches offers protection from hungry hawks. This is where she will build her nest.

The Kaibab Squirrel

The Kaibab squirrel has a jet-black belly and frosty white tail. The squirrel lives in the ponderosa forest on the North Rim of Grand Canyon and in the Kaibab National Forest north of the national park. Having darker fur on her belly helps the Kaibab squirrel absorb more of the sun's warmth during the cold winter season. Kaibab squirrels are special because they do not live anywhere else on Earth!

Soon Mother is busy clipping small branches from tree limbs and carrying them in her mouth to the nest site. She has no trouble chewing through the brown bark with her sharp teeth. Using her mouth and front paws, the squirrel weaves together branch after branch like the reeds of a basket. Her little nest begins to grow. When she finishes the nest, she fashions a roof with pine branches. The roof will keep out rain and snow.

The Abert's Squirrel

Abert's squirrels have a snow-white belly and glistening grayish tail. Using their large tails, Abert squirrels maintain their balance when they leap from one ponderosa to another. When they rest on pine branches during the day, they flip up their tails over their bodies like furry umbrellas, shading themselves from the sun. Abert's squirrels live in many of the ponderosa forests of the southwestern United States.

Mother climbs inside the nest.

Satisfied with her progress, she slips back out and runs down

the tree trunk. She startles a mountain chickadee, and the bird

quickly disappears into its nesting nook in the trunk.

The squirrel wants soft things to line the bottom of her new

home, so she gathers grasses, feathers, mosses, and even some

rabbit fur. When the soft bottom is finished, her nest is ready.

Wildflowers

During spring and summer, a colorful array of wildflowers

sprouts in the ponderosa forest. Many birds, insects, and

butterflies are attracted to the brightly

colored flowers for their nectar and

pollen. Pollination occurs when pollen

is carried from one flower to another by

birds and insects.

Finally, Mother climbs

to the top of the tree. A handsome Steller's jay is perched in a sunny spot nearby, but the bluish bird ignores her.

Her work is done, and she is hungry. She scampers to the tip of a branch to eat tender golden pollen cones, which are tiny, finger-shaped cones packed with pollen. As she nibbles, a mask of yellow powder settles on her whiskers and tiny black nose. Her hunger satisfied, Mother returns to her new home.

Nighttime Predators

At sunset, some ponderosa forest creatures active only at night make their appearance. Some of these animals are predators looking for other animals to eat for dinner. Owls, foxes, coyotes, and mountain lions must have good night vision to spot prey. Owls also use their keen sense of hearing to find a meal in the dark. They glide down on silent wings and catch dinner with their sharp talons.

Seed Cones and Pollen Cones

The large pinecones in ponderosas are seed cones.
As these cones develop, they are bright green. They turn
brown after they open and release their seeds.

Pollen cones are much smaller than seed cones.
They are filled with yellow pollen that is spread by
the wind. They grow only during May and June
of each year. They appear in clusters at the
tips of a ponderosa's branches.

After a night of sound sleep,

Mother pokes her head out of the nest. It is still

early. She sees a great horned owl fly silently

overhead. It is returning to a favorite daytime

perch to sleep. This nighttime-hunter will be

sleeping before Mother ventures

out in search of food.

A few days later, the soft nest contains three pink baby squirrels. They curl close to Mother and fill their bellies with her warm milk. Until their eyes and ears open, they depend on Mother to feed and protect them. They drink and drink. Two of the baby squirrels grow quickly. The third baby squirrel is too small and weak to survive. By the second week, the nest contains only two baby squirrels, Rascal and Little Brother.

Squirrel Development

Newborn tassel-eared squirrels are about two inches long (about as long as a key to your house), and they weigh about 1/2 ounce (about the weight of three nickels). The newborn squirrels' eyes and ears are closed, and they do not have any fur. They have tiny claws on their feet and soft whiskers on their faces. After a few weeks, soft fur develops. Mother squirrels nurse their babies for about ten weeks.

Summer

Mother nurses and protects her two babies. Early one morning, she hears something close to the nest. She looks outside.

A plump porcupine sits in the tree. Moving toward him, Mother barks and stomps her feet. The porcupine's stiff quills rise. Mother barks again and flicks her large tail. The porcupine swings his prickly tail. Even though she jumps backward, three sharp quills hit her nose. In spite of the pain, she holds her ground. The porcupine finds another tree.

When the danger is past, she strokes her forepaws against the quills until one comes out. She then brushes her nose against a branch, and the other two fall from her tender nose. She returns to her hungry babies.

Animal Defenses

All animals of the ponderosa forest must protect themselves and their babies from predators. Porcupines have sharp quills to keep away animals that want to eat them. Skunks have black fur with white stripes or spots. These two colors together are warning colors. When threatened, a skunk releases a bad-smelling, long-lasting spray. Horned lizards have skin colors similar to their surroundings. When a predator threatens, they remain very still and are hard to see. Rabbits have strong muscles in their legs, helping them run fast and change directions quickly. Bees and wasps use their stingers for protection.

Butterflies and Moths

Butterflies and moths are beautiful insects. Their delicate wings carry them from flower to flower, and their coiled tongues allow them to sip nectar. Some are a solid color while others have many colors, with stripes and other markings. Butterflies are easy to distinguish from moths. Most butterflies are out during the day, while moths are active at night. At rest, moths hold their wings outstretched while butterflies keep theirs folded. Butterflies and moths are important pollinators of the wildflowers in ponderosa forests.

Summer is warm and pleasant. It is time to explore. Rascal peeks out of the nest, adjusting her eyes to the sunshine. She is a curious little squirrel, and she ventures out first, followed by her brother. With Mother close by, both youngsters explore.

Rascal climbs out on a limb and selects a pine twig. She disturbs a butterfly, and it flutters gently away. The young squirrel peels away the dark outer bark of the twig. Rolling the twig in her front paws, Rascal eats the tender inner bark like corn-on-the-cob, dropping the white stick that remains. Little Brother tries a pine twig, too. Summer is going to be a great adventure.

Forest Beetles

Beetles come in many sizes and colors, and several kinds live in ponderosa forests. Some longhorn beetles feed on the tissues of living trees, and others feed on dead and decaying trees. A little heap of sawdust near a tree is, mostly likely, evidence that a longhorn beetle is nearby. Pine-bark beetles can sometimes be so plentiful that they can kill a tree. Ladybird beetles, sometimes called ladybugs, have small orange bodies with black dots. As the temperatures fall in autumn, you may see ladybird beetles gathering on tree trunks or on pinecones on the ground. They're seeking shelter from the coming winter in the cracks of the tree and inside the opened cones.

Soon, the two young

squirrels no longer need Mother's milk.

They grow bigger and stronger on the

abundant foods of the forest.

One day they are startled by a flock of

pygmy nuthatches feeding among the

branches of the nest tree. Rascal and her

brother watch as the birds probe for insects.

After a short time, the birds are on their

way, and the two little squirrels continue

exploring the ponderosa forest.

Several afternoons during the summer, clouds

gather in the sky. Heavy raindrops from monsoon storms pour

down. All three squirrels run to the shelter of their nest.

Lightning flashes and thunder booms. Far away, lightning strikes

a ponderosa. It catches fire and glows like a torch in the darkened

forest. The odor of smoke filters into the nest. Mother is alert,

sniffing the air. But before long, a heavy downpour douses the

flames. The squirrel family is dry and secure in the well-built nest.

Mother's calm reassures the little squirrels, and they curl close to

Tree Snags

After ponderosa trees are struck by lightning, or after they become infested with insects or with a fungus, they eventually die. Such standing dead trees are called snags. Some bat species roost under the loose bark of snags. Many insects feed on the dead wood. These insects attract woodpeckers. Bare limbs serve as perches or lookouts for eagles and hawks. Many birds, including mountain chickadees and three-toed woodpeckers, use ponderosa snags as nest sites. Some mammals, such as raccoons, squirrels, and gray foxes, also nest in tree cavities. Snags are vital to the health and survival of many species of wildlife in the forest.

One day Mother takes her two young squirrels to explore the forest floor. She knows that plump, tasty mushrooms spring from the soil after the rains. They quickly find some. As the two young squirrels watch, Mother snatches one and carries it up the tree. She places it on a branch to dry. Then Rascal plucks her own and bounds up the tree. She hangs it high in the branches just as Mother has done. Little Brother plucks mushrooms, too. The stored mushrooms will become winter meals.

Ponderosa Litter Layer

Ponderosas keep their needles for three years. The oldest green needles eventually turn brown. During the early fall, wind blows the brown needles from their branches, and they fall to the ground. Over the years, the ground layer of pine needles combined with branches and other dead plants can become very deep. This litter layer protects the ground from erosion and from drying out. Small insects and worms live just below the litter, feeding on the decomposing materials. When the thick litter layer dries out, it can become fuel for a forest fire.

One afternoon Rascal ventures

high into their nest tree and travels along

the spreading branches into neighboring

trees. She searches for tasty twigs and prickly

green pinecones. The squirrel leaps toward a

more distant tree, and her beautiful gray tail

twirls gracefully behind her. Oops! Rascal

misses the branch. The squirrel falls and

painfully hits the ground chest-first. All the

air is knocked out of her. Slowly, she lifts her

head to look around. She is in the middle

of a cluster of bright-purple asters and tall

forest grasses. But the ground is a dangerous

place for a little squirrel. Rascal pulls herself

together and scampers quickly up a tree.

Forest Grasses

Many grasses thrive beneath the immense ponderosas. Grasses have hardy root systems that help hold the soil together. When the winter's cold temperatures and snow-cover cause the tops of the grasses to die, the roots remain alive, insulated from the winter above. When spring arrives, new green blades of grass shoot upward, beginning the cycle anew.

Little Brother travels to the end of a limb where a cluster of

enticing green pinecones hangs on the tree. He plucks one

of the large, sticky cones and hurries back to his

perch near the tree's trunk. Moments

later, a shower of cone scales falls

to the ground as he eats the

pine seeds. After finishing

one cone, he goes back

for another. Finally full,

he carries a third cone

down the tree in his

mouth. He digs a hole and

buries the meal.

Rascal, watching from a nearby

branch, can't resist the temptation to steal

her brother's treasure. As soon as Little Brother

is gone, she digs up the cone and hides it in her own secret

place, then sprints back up the tree, satisfied with her clever trick.

Ponderosa Pinecone Cores

Ponderosa pinecones require more than two years to ripen. When the cones are in their final few months of growth, squirrels climb onto the tree branches to pluck them. Sometimes a squirrel will select a cone and begin to remove the scales. All of the cone's protective scales are discarded and fall to the forest floor. Once the scales are removed, the squirrel can quickly eat the energy-packed seeds. The seeds are loaded with proteins and fats, and they are one of the choice foods squirrels enjoy.

Fall

The early morning air is crisp and cold. Rascal's breath makes little frosty clouds. Her fur has thickened, and tiny black hairs sprout from the tips of her ears.

Rascal dashes up a tree trunk in a dizzying spiral. She wants to explore. Rascal has gotten better at leaping, and she bounds from one tree to the next. This is fun! Soon, she comes to a colorful grove of Gambel oak trees. Jumping for the nearest oak branch, she startles a family of acorn woodpeckers. They scatter noisily in all directions.

Forest Birds

Many birds live in the ponderosa forest. Nuthatches eat insects and spiders living in the thick, rust-colored bark. Red crossbills use their unusual beaks to pry open ponderosa seed cones. Broad-tailed hummingbirds locate red flowers and slip their long, pointed beaks inside to sip nectar. Robins, with their bright orange breasts, feed on insects that live amidst the grasses and shrubs growing from the forest floor. Western bluebirds perch on narrow grass stems to search for seeds and insects. So you can see, the ponderosa forest offers a supermarket of food choices to many different birds.

Oak leaves have turned shades of burgundy, rust, and gold.

Plump, green acorns hang in clusters, each one tucked into its

tight, buff-colored cap. A flock of turkeys scratches the

ground below, looking for acorns that have fallen.

They don't notice Rascal.

Rascal snips a green acorn from a cluster and

samples it. It's delicious! She has another and

another. One drops, and it is quickly snapped

up by a turkey hen.

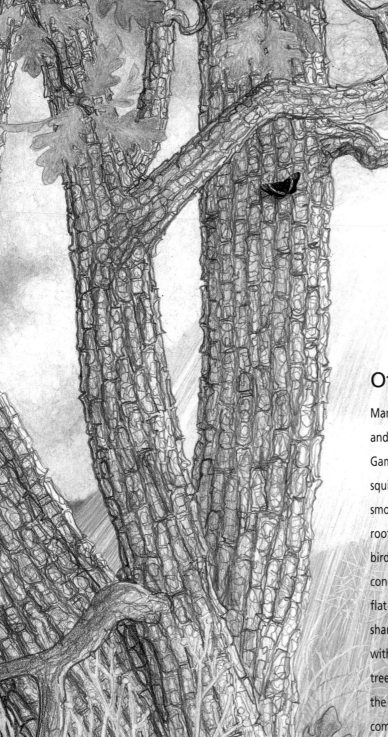

Other Trees

Many kinds of trees grow in a ponderosa forest, and they are very important to the forest's wildlife. Gambel oaks provide food for many animals, including squirrels, deer, and birds. Aspen trees, dressed in smooth white bark, send new shoots up from their roots. Pinyon trees produce sticky, sappy cones, but birds still feed on their seeds. Fir trees produce their cones near the top of the tree, and their needles are flat and soft to the touch. Spruce trees produce short, sharp needles. New Mexico locust trees are covered with elegant pink flowers in the spring. All of these trees provide perches, nest sites, shade, and foods for the many animals that live in the ponderosa forest community.

One sunny autumn afternoon, Rascal finds a mountain short-horned lizard basking in the sun on a warm rock. Rascal ignores the relaxed lizard; she has no time for such idleness. She buries pinecones and acorns in the loose soil of the forest floor. She tucks mushrooms here and there among pine branches. Mother and Little Brother hide their own treasures. Days are shorter, and nights are longer and colder. The hairs at the tips of her ears grow longer.

It is a busy time.

Mountain Short-Horned Lizard

The bodies of mountain short-horned lizards are covered with scales. Some of the scales stick up on the back of the lizard's head and look like horns. The horns give these lizards a fearsome look to predators. The lizards usually have skin colors similar to their environment, allowing them to hide from animals that might eat them.

Rascal scurries around

the bottom of a thick ponderosa. She stops

to sniff the soil. Her tiny black nose tells her

something good to eat is underneath the pine

needles, so she starts digging. Her small front

paws send dirt flying. There, attached to a

ponderosa root, she uncovers a false truffle, a

fungus that grows underground. The delicious

cream-colored false truffle is speckled with

dirt. Rascal bites into the rich brown center.

Yum! Close by, she uncovers another. What a

discovery!

Other Squirrel Foods

In addition to the energy-packed seeds inside ponderosa pinecones, tassel-eared squirrels eat many other things in the forest. They nibble tender, new mistletoe sprouts throughout the spring. They love to eat protein-rich pollen cones, which appear in the early summer. Later in the summer, as the rains begin, mushrooms send their pale stalks upward through the litter layer. Squirrels pluck mushrooms and then eat them on a nearby rock or pine stump. Like mushrooms, false truffles are more common when the forest soil is wet. Acorns are available in fall. During winter, tassel-eared squirrels rely on stored treasures and the inner bark of twigs.

While eating her tasty false truffles,

Rascal hears the rustle of dry grass and crushed leaves. Rascal stops feeding and looks up cautiously.

Close by, a mule deer buck nips golden leaves from an aspen tree. His tall forked antlers stir the leaves above him as he reaches higher. Leaves drift to the ground. Rascal has never seen such a massive creature.

Suddenly scared, Rascal leaps for the trunk of a ponderosa. She climbs until she is at eye level with the deer. The deer turns his head slowly toward the squirrel. Rascal barks at the intruder and scampers higher up in the tree. Looking down from a safer distance, she barks again and stomps her front feet. Ignoring the squirrel, the deer turns away and disappears into the forest.

Forest Mammals

Smaller mammals that share the same forest habitat with squirrels like Rascal include mice, pocket gophers, and voles. Several species of bats, the only flying mammals, live in the forest. Larger mammals such as the jackrabbit, striped skunk, raccoon, porcupine, gray fox, deer, and elk also make their homes in or near the ponderosa forest.

Rascal is nearly full-grown,

and she is plump from the many foods of the forest.

Her ears have tall, black tufts, just like Mother's. Rascal

scampers back through the cluster of old pines until she

reaches the nest tree. Pine needles stir in the gusty wind.

The air is turning chilly. She hurries up the tree and

settles into the warm nest.

Ponderosa Needles

Trees that do not shed their leaves in the fall are called evergreen trees. Needles are long, narrow leaves. Ponderosa needles grow in bundles of three. Each year new needles grow at the tip of a branch. After three years, the oldest needles turn brown and drop from the tree. The brown needles fall to the forest floor where they accumulate as leaf litter.

Ponderosa Seeds

Ponderosa seeds develop inside a seed cone. After two years, the cones open and release tiny winged seeds. The wing permits the little seed to spiral toward the ground, like a helicopter. Sometimes, wind carries the seeds far away from the parent tree. Once on the ground, some of the seeds are eaten by hungry animals such as jays, mice, and chipmunks. When spring arrives the next year, the seeds that weren't eaten may germinate and push up tiny green sprouts from the forest floor.

As the weeks go by, the forest changes a little each day. Strong afternoon winds pull free the old brown needles of the ponderosa, and they fall. They make a stiff, tan carpet on the forest floor.

Tightly closed green pinecones turn brown and open, releasing their tiny winged seeds. Rascal watches as these seeds spin in circles on their journey to the ground.

The forest floor is not as soft as it was in summer. Flowers and butterflies are gone. Rascal notices all these changes. She's changing, too. Her fur thickens and her ear tufts grow longer.

Rascal scouts for the perfect tree

in which to build her own nest. She finds a

sheltered tree in a cluster of other pines and

starts building. Rascal works hard on her nest,

one as sturdy as Mother's. When she finishes,

she is pleased with her new home.

Rascal is hungry after working so hard, so she

clips pine twigs. She turns them skillfully in her

front paws, stripping the outer bark. After eating

the inner layer of several twigs, Rascal crawls

into her nest for her first night alone. Nest

building is a big job, and she is ready to sleep.

Squirrel Nests

Squirrels build their nests either on branches near the tops or in forks in ponderosa trunks. The round nests are built of woven pine branches. The entrances to the nests usually face south and east to capture as much warmth from the sun as possible. A single squirrel usually builds several nests. Occasionally, cavities in oak trees are used for nests.

Winter

A light blanket of fallen snow covers the ground when Rascal crawls from her snug bed to greet the rising winter sun. She scampers down her nest tree. On the ground, the squirrel sniffs until she smells a buried pinecone. She sends snow flying with her busy front paws. Sure enough, there it is. Rascal carries her meal with her teeth until finding a sunny, sheltered perch where she can eat the seeds.

Rascal discovers she can scamper about easily on the hard-crusted snow after a cold night. The squirrel smells a false truffle with her sensitive nose and digs through the frosty crust to find it. Retrieving her treasure, she finds a safe place to enjoy it.

False Truffles

Both false truffles and true truffles are
underground fungi that live on tree
roots. Squirrels eat false truffles;
humans eat true truffles. False
truffles are important to the growth
of ponderosas because, like tiny
sponges, they soak up and store water and soil nutrients,
which are passed along to the tree. False truffles receive
nutrients from the tree also. Squirrels spread
false-truffle spores throughout the forest
in their droppings.

Airborne Predators

Two raptors feed on squirrels. Red-tailed hawks swoop down on unwary squirrels feeding in the sunny openings of ponderosa forests. Northern goshawks, which have short wings, can fly between trees and feed on preoccupied squirrels on the shady forest floor. Goshawks drop from their perches on tree branches, flap their powerful, silent wings two or three times, and glide in on unsuspecting squirrels.

Little Brother sits on a log, nibbling on a pinecone, when a shadow suddenly sweeps toward him. Mother, not far away, lets out a warning bark. A silent goshawk dives before Little Brother can react. Rascal watches helplessly as the goshawk lifts Little Brother and carries him away in its sharp talons.

Now Rascal is the only little squirrel left. She flees in fright toward Mother, but soon remembers her own nest. She climbs quickly up her tree to safety.

Winter Survival

As winter approaches, forest animals change in
order to survive. Western spade-foot toads dig into
the soil and hibernate. Tassel-eared squirrels, rabbits, elk, and deer grow thicker
and, sometimes, darker fur. They also remain active during the winter, looking
for plants growing above or beneath the snow cover. Skunks move into dens and
remain inactive for weeks at a time, venturing out only in warmer weather to feed.
Mice and voles stay underground in snug burrows, feeding on stored seeds.
Hummingbirds and many other birds migrate to warmer climates and
return in late spring.

When Rascal comes out again, the sun has warmed and softened the snow. She searches for pinecones buried near the tree but each time she bounds, she sinks into the cold white fluff. Rascal continues to bound and sink, as if she were swimming through the snow.

It is hard work.

She returns to her tree to nibble on twigs. Sometimes snowstorms last longer than a day. Chilled robins fluff their feathers for warmth. Food is difficult to find as the snow deepens, but pine twigs are always available for Rascal to eat.

Rascal stays curled up inside her nest to keep warm. Some animals hibernate now, but Rascal has to eat almost every day. Her thick fur and fluffy ear tufts protect her body and ears from the cold.

When she ventures out to find food, snowflakes fall on her soft, furry back. Rascal discovers an elk antler sticking up out of the snow. She gnaws on it.

Soon the snow begins to stick to Rascal's fur. Her back and head start to turn white. She runs toward home, shaking off her snowy coat.

Deer and Elk Antlers

Male deer and elk eat a lot of vegetation to help grow their antlers. Males use their antlers to push and shove each other during the mating season. Usually, one of the males eventually grows tired of sparring and leaves. The remaining male mates with the available females.

After mating season, deer and elk shed antlers, which fall to the forest floor. Since squirrels have teeth that grow throughout their lives, they gnaw on antlers to keep their teeth sharp and short, and to get calcium, a necessary nutrient for good health.

Rascal hears a peck-peck-pecking

sound above her. A tiny white-breasted nuthatch searches for insects

and spiders under the tree bark. Rascal doesn't move while the

upside-down bird nibbles closer and closer. Rascal tilts her

head and flicks her bushy tail. The startled nuthatch flies

away, and Rascal races back to her nest.

White-Breasted, Red-Breasted, and Pygmy Nuthatches

Nuthatches are tiny, comical birds. They scramble
down a tree trunk headfirst to search for spiders and insects
that live in the cracks of bark. All three kinds of nuthatches live in
conifer forests, including ponderosa pine, spruce, and fir forests. In areas
with very cold winters, nuthatches move south, but in areas where winters
are milder, they feed by looking for hibernating insects.

Slowly, days grow longer.

The snow melts, and new green sprouts push through

the forest litter. New pine needles and tiny pollen cones

develop on the tips of ponderosa branches. Rascal is not as

plump as she had been when the winter storms set in. She used

the fat she had made over the summer and fall for energy

to stay warm during the cold winter.

Rascal stretches in the soothing glow of the sun. It feels

wonderful. She dashes happily along the familiar highway

of pine branches. It is a beautiful day. Rascal will soon

build a new nest and raise her own family among the

tall ponderosas of Grand Canyon National Park.

The Ranges of Abert's and Kaibab Squirrels

Abert's sqirrels live on the South Rim of Grand Canyon, as well as in the ponderosa pine forests in other parts of Arizona, New Mexico, Colorado, and Utah. Kaibab squirrels live on the North Rim of Grand Canyon and in the portion of the Kaibab National Forest north of the canyon.

Other Squirrels of the Grand Canyon Region

Squirrels are rodents, a type of mammal with front teeth that are constantly growing. Females provide milk for their young. Their relatives include, mice, rats, marmots, lemmings, muskrats, gophers, beavers, and voles. Here are some other squirrels that live in the Grand Canyon region.

Gunnison's prairie dogs live in towns of burrows connected with tunnels. Prairie dogs are sometimes found in open, sandy areas on the South Rim. They also live in other parts of the southwestern United States. They feed on grasses and other plants.

Several species of chipmunks live at Grand Canyon and in other parts of the western United States. They make their homes in ponderosa forests, oak forests, pastures, and sagebrush deserts.

Golden-mantled ground squirrels look like chubby chipmunks without stripes on their faces. At Grand Canyon, they can be found on the North Rim. These ground squirrels also live in other parts of the western United States. They eat pine seeds, mushrooms, and fruits.

Chickarees are noisy bundles of energy that can be found on the North Rim. These small, red squirrels live in spruce, fir, pine, and mixed-hardwood forests. They live from northern Arizona north to Alaska, and in many cold climates of North America. Chickarees store pinecones in large piles, called middens. They save them for winter.

Rock squirrels are ground squirrels that burrow in rock crevices. They live on both sides of the Grand Canyon. They have rust-colored speckles on their backs. They are almost as large as Rascal, but their tails are not fluffy. They eat berries and various seeds.

The tiny white-tailed antelope squirrel can be found on the South Rim and in the canyon. It has white stripes on tawny-gray sides. The underside of the tail is white. It eats the seeds and fruits of various plants.

The spotted ground squirrel lives on the South Rim. It has brown fur with spots on its back. It feeds on seeds, fruits, and, sometimes, insects.

Rascal has many interesting Grand Canyon relatives on both the South and North rims.

About the Author

Sylvester Allred is a biology professor at Northern Arizona University in Flagstaff, where he has studied tassel-eared squirrels for over twenty years. He is the author of *The Forest Alphabet Encyclopedia* and *The Desert Alphabet Encyclopedia*. He lives with his wife, Donna, in the ponderosa forest near the base of Mount Humphreys.

About the Artist

Diane Iverson is the author and/or illustrator of several children's nature books and a popular speaker at elementary schools. She has also illustrated several books for adults. Diane and her husband, Doug, live just outside Prescott, Arizona, at the edge of Granite Mountain Wilderness Area.